This book belongs to:
10
MB
MB

Published by Bendon Publishing International, Ashland, OH 44805

Printed in China

Piggy Visits the Doctor

by Ellen Weiss illustrated by Kathy Spahr

Today was the day for Piggy's checkup at the doctor's office.

"Come on in, Piggy," said Dr. Brown.

"Can my doll come, too?" asked Piggy.

"Sure!" said the doctor. "What's her name?"

"Lemonade," said Piggy. "I'm going to give her a checkup, too."

"That's fine," said Dr. Brown.

Nanny helped Piggy take off her clothes and put them down on a chair.

"First we'll check your height and weight," said the doctor. "Let's see...you weigh forty pounds and you're forty inches tall."

Then the doctor turned to the baby-weighing scale. "Lemonade," she said, "weighs one and a half pounds. That's very good."

"Can you hop up onto the table for me, Piggy?" asked Dr. Brown.

Piggy got up on the big table. The paper was crinkly.

"Now I'm going to listen to your heartbeat with my stethoscope, first on your front and then on your back. Take a nice, deep breath, please," said Dr. Brown.

"It's cold and tickly," said Piggy. Then she picked up Lemonade.

"Your turn, Lemonade," said Piggy. "Take a deep breath."

"Next we'll look into your ears," said the doctor. "We need to see if there are any bunny rabbits in there."

"Bunny rabbits!" giggled Piggy. "I don't have any bunny rabbits in my ears!"

"And now we'll look down your throat. Can you stick out your tongue at me and say 'Aaah'?"

Piggy had lots of fun saying "aaah" to the doctor.

"You, too, Lemonade," said Piggy. "Can you stick out your tongue at me and say 'Aaah'?"

"Now comes a funny part," said Dr. Brown. "I'm going to tap your knee with this little rubber hammer and see if your kicker works okay."

Boing! Piggy's kicker worked just fine.

"It's time to feel your tummy," said the doctor. "Can you lie down on your back?"

"Now I'm going to feel *your* tummy, Lemonade," said Piggy. "Doesn't that tickle?"

"It's time for your booster shot, Piggy, so you'll stay nice and healthy. Can you be very brave? It will just be a quick little pinprick, and then we'll be all done."

Lemonade was very brave for her shot, too.

"You're all done, Piggy," said the doctor. "You were a great patient. What kind of present would you like from the toy jar?"

Piggy picked out a nice necklace for herself.

And since Lemonade had been such a good patient, too, she got a present as well. A Piggy-size bracelet made a very nice Lemonade-size necklace!

A
DOG